HOORAY FOR TODAY!

Words and pictures by

Brian Won

Houghton Mifflin Harcourt
Boston • New York

For all the parents who've wished their wide-awake child would just *go to sleep.*

Library of Congress Cataloging-in-Publication Data is available.

ISBN 978-0-544-74803-3

Manufactured in China

SCP 10 9 8 7 6 5 4 3 2 1

4500595649

"I'm wide awake and
ready to play!" said Owl.
"This will be a good, good day."

She packed her toys
and set off to find her friends.

Owl knocked on Elephant's door.

"HOORAY FOR TODAY!

I have my hat.

Would you like to play?"

But Elephant did not want to play.

"NOT NOW.
I'M SLEEPY!"

So Owl tucked Elephant back in
and whispered, "Maybe another day.
Good night, Elephant."

Then Owl found Zebra.

"HOORAY FOR TODAY!

I have my trumpet.
Would you like to play?"

But Zebra did not want to play.

"NOT NOW. I'M SLEEPY!"

So Owl tooted a lullaby
and whispered, "Maybe another day.
Sleep tight, Zebra."

Then Owl found Turtle.

"HOORAY FOR TODAY!

I have balloons.
Would you like to play?"

But Turtle did not want to play.

"NOT NOW.
I'M SLEEPY!"

So Owl rocked Turtle to sleep
and whispered, "Maybe another day.
Sweet dreams, Turtle."

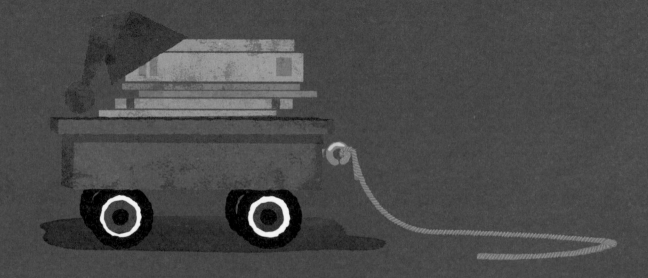

Then Owl found Giraffe.

"HOORAY FOR TODAY!

I have some books.

Would you like to play?"

But Giraffe did not want to play.

"NOT NOW.
I'M SLEEPY!"

So Owl read a story
and whispered, "Maybe another day.
Nighty-night, Giraffe."

When Owl found Lion, she couldn't hoot
a single word before Lion growled,

"NOT NOW.

I'M SLEEPY!"

So Owl whispered, "Maybe another day.
Rest well, Lion," and tiptoed away.

Owl shouted into the night.

"HOO-HOO-HOO

RAY

FOR TODAY!

Can anyone come out to play?"

"Today is a bad, bad day," Owl said.
"Nobody wants to play!"

Finally, as the sun came up,
she walked back home . . .

. . . where her friends were waiting.

"Good morning, Owl!" they all shouted.

"Would you like to play?"

Owl yawned.

"NOT NOW. I'M SLEEPY!

But after my nap . . .

HOORAY!
LET'S PLAY!"